D1561135

It Wasn't Tradition

By A. Intisar Turner

For my mother, Jacqueline,
for her life long inspiration and community work.

To little girls worldwide who will become great women.
Special thanks to my son, LightSpeed Ent.,
Larell, all my nieces, and my sisters.

Copyright 2014

Artwork by A. Intisar Turner
Illustration copyright 2014
Text copyright 2014

Library of Congress Cataloging-in-Publication Data

Turner, A. Intisar
It wasn't tradition / A. Intisar Turner; illustrated by A. Intisar Turner

ISBN 9780615996950

Visit:www.itwasnttradition.com

There once was a beautiful butterfly
who loved to adorn,

her wings with gold,
it was her favorite to be worn.

Being beautiful was lovely,
but that is not why she was born.

So one day she decided to fly.

Tradition taught her that women
were meant to be beautiful,
while the men got to fly.

Although it wasn't tradition,
she wanted to try.

The women were told
their wings were too weak.

Or if they took flight,
they might end up inside a bird's beak.

Tradition restricted women
to crawl through life as if they were
still in caterpillar form.

And if you challenged the system,
your wings could get clipped.
At a certain age, her wings fully ripped.

Forced to carry the burden of beauty
attached to her back.
Though her wings were a gift of life and freedom
understanding most lacked.

Yet one brave woman, I mean...butterfly,
decided to question tradition by asking them, "Why?"

"Where is your proof that
I am not meant to fly?"

She told them,
"Keep your oppressive tradition,

I'd much rather die."

Some found her spirit crazy,
yet somewhat amusing

While most felt
she was
disrespectful
and just
causing confusion.

Influencing others to challenge the law.

A menace to society,
that's what they saw.

So the leaders decided to silence her spirit.
But their systems and lies,
she just didn't fear it.

She continued to share her insight,
on how all butterflies
should be allowed to take flight.

The leaders plotted that night,

to clip her wings while she slept
to prevent her from flight.

They tied her down,
but not without a fight.

Most stood back and watched on,
even those who knew she was right.

She shivered in fear
as they approached her wings with the shears.

Some looked on with mean stares,
as she pleaded for help and shed tears.

As they proceeded with cutting her wing,

she prayed deep inside a miracle
the angels would bring.

They looked at each other in disbelief and said...

To their surprise,
all of her gold prevented the cut.

But still, it left a large wound.

Then they banned her from flying
and sentenced her back inside her cocoon.

Yet they could not break her spirit inside.

She spread out her wings and opened them wide.

She emerged with faith in her heart
and turned her wings to the wind.
They knew not where she was going,
but she looked determined.

It was a sight to remember,
her wings full of glitter and shine.
Poised in immaculate beauty,
her wings looked divine.

One asked,
"Is she really going to fly?"
Another said,
"Pass me a tissue,
I'm going to cry."

Some pleaded,
"Don't jump! You don't have a chance."

In the midst of their warning,

she stepped off the branch.

At first, it looked like she just fell.
But as they watched on, she flew very well.

She loved her freedom and flight,
it felt heaven bound.

Until she lost all control

and crashed to the ground.

It hurt, she was embarrassed,
but it wasn't the end.
She didn't give up, she just blamed the wind.

And she could care less what others said.
Some watched in support,
while some thought, "Surely she's dead."

But still, she got up
and she tried flight again.

But this time, she removed her gold
and turned her back to the wind.

The wind carried her
where she was meant to go.
Instead of diving face first, she rode it real slow.

She flew from big cities to poor little towns,
and helped pollinate every flower she found.

And she would have flown
to the end of the earth,
if it was not round.

And up to the sky,

if the flowers she loved

were not so close to the ground.

She proved to them all
that some traditions are wrong.

The more she took flight,
the more her wings grew strong.

And guess what?
She never lost her beauty.

It just enhanced
as she fulfilled her life's duty.

As her wings grew strong,
she was able to put her gold back on.

And other women decided
to take flight too.
It wasn't tradition,
it was the right thing to do.

The End.